CLAN CASTLES

EVAN JACOBS

SADDLEBACK
EDUCATIONAL PUBLISHING

red rhino
bOOks®

Body Switch	The Hero of	Sky Watchers
The Cat Whisperer	Crow's Crossing	The Soldier
Clan Castles	Home Planet	Space Trip
The Code	I Am Underdog	Standing by Emma
Fight School	Killer Flood	Starstruck
Fish Boy	Little Miss Miss	Stolen Treasure
Flyer	The Lost House	Too Many Dogs
The Garden Troll	The Love Mints	World's Ugliest Dog
Ghost Mountain	The Magic Stone	Zombies!
The Gift	Out of Gas	Zuze and the Star
	Racer	

With more titles on the way …

SADDLEBACK
EDUCATIONAL PUBLISHING
www.sdlback.com

ISBN-13: 978-1-62250-921-8
ISBN-10: 1-62250-921-8
eBook: 978-1-63078-047-0

Printed in Guangzhou, China
NOR/1015/CA21501444

19 18 17 16 15   2 3 4 5 6

KING NOJRA

Age: 35

Family: a mean older sister who rules a neighboring castle

Secret Wish: to live in the world outside his video game

Favorite Hobby: cake decorating

Best Quality: great hair

CHARACTERS

JAKE

Age: 11

Favorite Food: Hot Pockets ham & cheese

Second Favorite Hobby: enjoys taking photographs of funny-looking bugs

Secret He's Keeping: has a crush on Olivia, the girl who sits behind him in art class

Best Quality: persistence

1
UNLOCKED

"You boys better get in bed. Right now!"

Jake's mother was mad. She already told them to go to sleep. That was two hours ago. But Jake and his best friend, Kyle, kept playing.

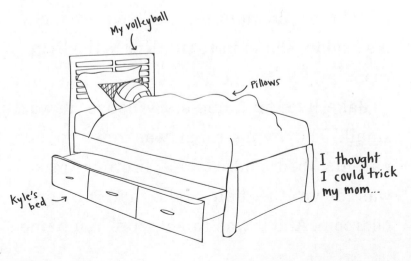

My volleyball

Pillows

I thought I could trick my mom...

Kyle's bed →

"Three more minutes, Mom. I promise," Jake said. "We're almost done. We're at level ninety-eight!"

"Three more minutes. You boys are lucky it's Friday." She shut to the door to the living room.

Jake lived in a one-story house. It was small. The living room was next to his parents' bedroom. Jake's brother, Mike, was down the hall. Jake had his own bedroom. And it was full of stuff. You name it. He had it. Games. Comic books. DVDs. Electronics.

Jake and Kyle had been on the Xbox all night. They always played when Kyle slept over. They were seconds away from clearing Level 99 of their favorite game. It was called *Clan Castles*.

They battled a king at each level. Winning meant they won the king's castle. The final battle was against King Nojra. That king was the fiercest. The bravest. And the scariest.

King Nojra was half-man, half-dragon. He ruled the biggest kingdom. If you lost to him, you lost it all. And you were bumped back to Level 1.

KING NOJRA

comes off pretty classy

Calm King Nojra, before he gets mad.

constantly shines his shoes

Jake's avatar and King Nojra were fighting. Nojra was throwing fireballs. Giant creatures were on the attack. The king's great hall was a war zone. The other kings were watching. The ones Jake and Kyle had beaten. It had taken the boys months to get to this level.

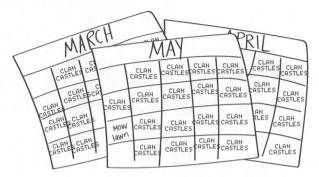

"If you die, it's over," Kyle said.

"Don't remind me," Jake moaned.

King Nojra was using all his skills. Jake had to be fast. He had to move and fire at the same time. The king kept at it. Faster. And faster. If Jake blinked, he lost.

Then, the game made a sound.

"What's going on?" Kyle asked.

At that moment, the Mirror of Reflection appeared. It sat off to the side. A counter appeared on the screen. It was counting down from five.

"I only have five seconds to get it!" Jake was so tense. He was sweating.

If he did not get the mirror, it would disappear. Forever.

Too much was coming at him. Jake was stuck.

Suddenly, he got a break. For a split second. There was an opening. Jake took it.

Two seconds left.

Jake grabbed the mirror.

Nojra spit out a fireball.

Fireballs

"Lift it!" Kyle yelled.

Jake did.

The fireball bounced off the mirror. It shot back into Nojra's body.

The Mirror of Reflection

HEY! Is that my volleyball?

Direct hit!

King Nojra vanished. There was a white light.

The screen went black.

"Whoa! You beat ninety-nine." Kyle put his arm around Jake.

"Now what?" Jake asked.

The screen was still black. The boys waited. It was dead quiet.

Then many colors filled the TV screen. Every king Jake had battled and defeated appeared.

"Cool," Jake said.

The screen read:

MOVE CLOSER
TO SEE ALL YOU HAVE WROUGHT
— KING N.

The boys did.

A white light shot out of the TV! The same light as when King Nojra vanished.

Jake and Kyle looked at each other.

"We're moving!" Jake yelled.

They were.

In seconds, colors surrounded them.

The TV had sucked them in!

2
INSIDE

Jake and Kyle landed on their feet. They both had backpacks.

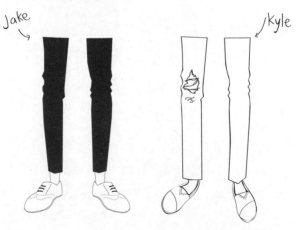

Jake

Kyle

They were inside the game! They had played *Clan Castles* a million times. But this was different.

They felt small.

The tall castles. Each a different color. Green hills in between. People in the distance.

"Are those robbers?" Kyle asked.

"Yes," Jake said. He could see farther than in the "real world." Probably video-game vision. "I think they are."

All around them they heard talking. The kings of the kingdom! They always spoke as one. The kings spoke to the poor villagers.

The villagers cheered. They had to. If not, they got in trouble. They paid a fine. Or they went to jail.

"Jake." Kyle sounded scared. "What's going on? How did we get here?"

"I guess by clearing that level." Jake wasn't afraid. He was excited.

Jake looked around. He saw food. He saw gold. They needed these things. They needed them to complete their mission. To win.

"Where are you going?" Kyle yelled.

Jake walked to the gold. He grabbed some. It was floating in the air. Easy! He put it in his backpack.

"We need this stuff. Remember?" Jake smiled.

Jake grabbed a sandwich. He tore it in half. He gave half to Kyle.

FLYING SUBS

"I don't know about this, Jake. We need to get out of here. We need to be gone. Quick! Before the robbers see us."

"We love playing this game!" Jake smiled.

He took a huge bite of sandwich. Chewed. Swallowed. "Now we're inside. Hey, eat your sandwich. It's so good. The best!"

"How do we get out?" Kyle was worried.

Jake looked into the distance. Once again, his super vision kicked in. He saw all ninety-nine castles. "Awesome," he whispered. He looked at Kyle. "Looks like we keep playing."

3
CASTLE 1

"It took us months to clear all ninety-nine castles." Kyle was freaking out. "We can't stay here that long!"

Suddenly, a robber got closer. A lot closer.

There it is again!

Jake didn't see the robber. "What choice do we have? Besides, maybe time is different here."

"Uh, Jake …"

Jake was too busy staring at all the castles. He was trying to think. How had they cleared each one?

"Jake!" Kyle yelled.

A robber came toward them. He was huge. His beard was bushy and black. And he was swinging a chain. At the end of it was a ball. A steel ball. Full of spikes.

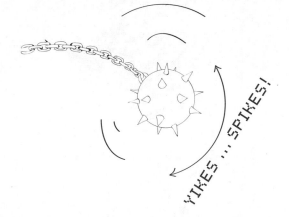

YIKES … SPIKES!

"What happens if he hits us with that?" Kyle asked.

The boys took off toward the first castle.

"Let's not find out!" Jake cried.

Since *Clan Castles* was a kids' game, nobody died. If you lost, you started over. Level 1. That would suck.

They crossed a wobbly bridge. The first castle was ahead. The wobbly bridge creaked. And cracked. It was falling apart!

CREAK CREAK CREAK CRACK CRACK CRACK

"Jake, you're crazy," Kyle cried. "We can't play this game. Not for real. No way!"

Duckanhas from the pond below jumped up. Half-duck, half-piranha. With huge teeth. They snapped at the boys.

Jake and Kyle both screamed. The duckanhas just missed them. Their teeth were sharp.

They entered the first castle.

"Ahhh!" the robber yelled. He was still behind them.

The boys turned. The bridge had broken. The robber fell into the duckanhas pond.

"Don't look! Let's keep going." Jake pulled Kyle into the castle.

"Jake," Kyle yelled. "I hate you!"

Next came a flying bat attack. Then they moved through giant cobwebs. And dodged flaming arrows.

Finally, they found the king. High in the castle. Someone had warned his sentry.

The sentry was firing cannonballs. At them!

Boom!

Bits of bricks flew everywhere. Jake and Kyle hid under a table.

"We need to distract him!" Jake yelled.

"We need to get out of here!" Kyle looked for an escape. There! An opening to the king's room.

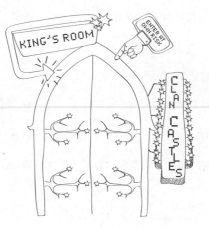

Jake spotted some broken bricks. He had an idea.

"Kyle, cover me!" Jake ran out from under the table.

"With what?" Kyle screamed.

The sentry aimed his cannon at Jake.

Kyle stood. "Over here, you big dummy!" he yelled.

The sentry got confused. He didn't know where to aim.

Jake seized the moment. He picked up some bricks. He stuffed them into the cannon. Then he took off.

The sentry smiled. He had Jake in his sights. He fired. The sentry did not know about the bricks. The cannonball got stuck.

It exploded!

Wham! The sentry smashed into a wall. Then fell to the ground.

At this point, the king threw up his arms. He had lost.

"You have defeated the first castle." Tears rolled down his cheeks. "I give up. I will give everybody more land, food, and money."

"That wasn't so hard." Jake held up his hand for Kyle to high-five.

"Not hard? We almost got killed!" Kyle stated. He was mad.

"Well, only ninety-eight more to go." Jake put his hand down.

Trumpets sounded. A chariot pulled up below. The boys ran down the castle steps. They climbed on. Inside were food, gold, and clubs.

4
LEVELING UP

Later, the boys were at Level 8. Eight castles in. This was the most intense game of *Clan Castles* ever.

So far, they had swung on a giant rope.

They'd fought with some angry skeletons.

They were chased by a *boarwolf*. Half-boar, half-wolf.

BOARWOLF

And they'd even gone over a waterfall.

Somehow, Jake and Kyle were still in one piece.

Now, they were fighting a *minagon*. Half-minotaur, half-dragon. It was ten feet tall. It had a horse's body. And a dragon's head. It was green and brown. And covered in scales.

The minagon had trapped them. They couldn't move. The castle wall was on one side. The minagon was on the other. It was breathing fire. The heat was too close to their heads. Their hair crackled.

smells like burnt hair

"Remember what I told you? About not wanting to die," Kyle cried.

More fire. More heat.

"We're not gonna die," Jake yelled. "We can't. It's a game." He had told Kyle this a hundred times.

Kyle eyed the minagon. Around its neck, he saw a key. It was silver. And huge. Bigger than any key he had ever seen. "Jake! The key. The key," he yelled.

The fire was too hot. Kyle moved his face

away. The monster got even closer.

"We're gonna die!" Kyle was over it. He was over *Clan Castles*. He wanted to be back in the real world. Where it was safe. Where monsters weren't real.

Jake grabbed his *sworderang*. A combo sword and boomerang. It was Jake's favorite weapon when he played this game.

The minagon moved. Just a hair. Jake threw the sworderang. It cut the rope holding the key. It dropped to the floor.

The sworderang came back again. The minagon ducked.

Jake caught the weapon.

The minagon looked up. It puffed more fire. Then it spread its wings. And flew away.

Jake and Kyle watched it in awe.

"Why'd it do that? It never did that before." Kyle was stunned.

"You want me to call it back? I can have it breathe more fire in your face." Jake laughed.

"No. Way."

Jake picked up the key. It unlocked all the doors in the castle. At least that was how it worked before.

Jake ran up the castle stairs.

"Come on!" he called. "You wanna get home, right?"

Kyle followed his best friend.

5
NEW WORLD

Level 50. Phew! In the real world, it took weeks to get here. Inside the game? Maybe thirty minutes. Or so it seemed.

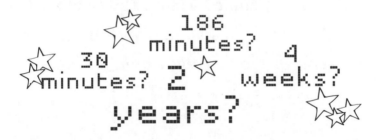

At that moment, they weren't thinking about time. Or anything else. The boys had run into a room. The king was here.

It had been so easy. Too easy.

A giant sentry appeared. Now they were trapped!

The sentry rushed toward them. His feet pounded on the old castle floor. This made the whole building shake.

Jake smiled at Kyle. He took out his sworderang. And threw it at the sentry. Jake loved using it. The weapon had been a lifesaver.

The sentry smiled. He hit the sworderang. Like it was a pesky bug. It fell. Useless. The sentry's smile grew wider.

Pesky Buggers!

"I told you. You use that too much!" Kyle eyed the sentry with fear.

Then Jake saw a small bag on a table. It looked useless. An unskilled player would never notice it. But Jake did.

"Bombs! We get them at this level." He grinned.

The sentry was a few feet away.

Jake grabbed the bag. He lifted it up high.

The sentry reached for the boys.

Jake threw the bag to the castle floor. Hard.

Thud!

At first, nothing happened.

"You're mine!" The sentry showed pointy teeth.

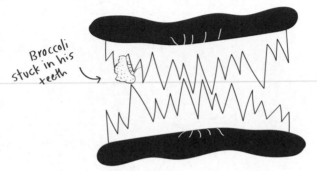

Broccoli stuck in his teeth →

The bag exploded!

Ka-boom!

The sentry fell back. He hit the castle wall. And went through it!

The castle was tall. The boys did not hear him hit the ground.

"You did it, Jake!" Kyle could not believe it. They fist-bumped.

A loud sound filled the air. Neither boy

had ever heard anything so loud.

The castle started to shake. A lot. It rocked. Back and forth. Back and forth.

The king lost his balance. He was rolling toward the hole the sentry had made. Then he was gone.

"I don't remember this in the game," Jake cried.

The boys tried to hold on. But they couldn't. Everything was moving.

"Jake," Kyle began. "I really want to stop playing now."

"Me too!"

Then the castle stopped shaking. Everything got very quiet.

"That wasn't so bad. Right?" Jake smiled.

They heard a low noise. It was working its way up. From the ground to the highest tower. It sounded like bricks. How could that be? Bricks popping out of the castle. The sound was getting louder. And louder.

The castle was crumbling!

Pop! Pop! Pop! Bricks went flying!

"We need to get out of here," Kyle screamed.

"We don't have time," Jake cried.

The floor crumbled under them. Every inch of the castle was breaking. Falling to the ground.

So were Jake and Kyle!

They were so high up. They seemed to fall forever. There was a lot of dust. They couldn't see anything. They just knew they were going down.

"Ahhh!" they both yelled.

They expected to hit the ground at any second.

Nobody died in *Clan Castles*.

But they had never been inside it. Only outside. Looking in.

What was going to happen next? Would they live? Or die?

Eventually, they stopped moving.

The bricks were gone. The dust was gone.

There was a little light.

Jake looked around. In the distance he saw a torch. It was on a wall.

They were no longer in a castle.

They were in a cave!

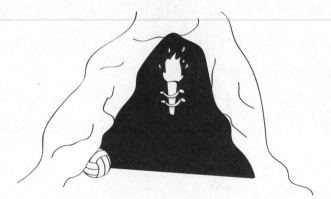

6
THE CAVES OF NOJRA

Jake and Kyle looked around. They were in a new part of the game. A part they had never seen.

Slowly their eyes adjusted to the dim light. They were in a cave maze. Lined with torches. Light glowed off the shiny walls.

Jake took it in. A memory flashed in his mind. A YouTube walk-through came to him. He saw it a while ago. Late at night. That was why he didn't recall it right away.

"Where are we?" Kyle wondered. He poked his head into another cave.

"I think this is that cave maze. The one we always hear about." Jake was beaming. "The Secret Caves of Nojra. I saw it on YouTube last month. It's a shortcut. We can be done. It's super fast. We can skip all the other castles!"

"We just have to find the right cave. Then we skip the other levels." Kyle was excited too. "We can get out of here! Go home!"

"Yeah. We just have to make the right guess. Then win the ninety-ninth level. Again," Jake said.

He knew it wasn't going to be easy. *Clan Castles* had pulled them in for a reason. What was it? Jake did not want to tell Kyle his worries. He did not want to upset him. They were going to have to earn their way out. Big-time.

"Which one?" Kyle asked.

"The one we can see the most of. The one with more light." Jake peeked into each cave. Kyle did too.

After about five minutes, they picked two.

"Which do you think?" Jake asked.

"Which do *you* think?" Kyle replied.

Jake stared at the two caves. Which seemed brighter?

"We're gonna need a torch." Kyle reached for one. He grabbed it by the handle. He turned it slightly. "If we get lost—"

Suddenly, the ground opened up below him.

Kyle was gone. Swallowed up by the ground.

GONE!

"Kyle!" Jake screamed. He could not believe what he was seeing.

The hole was gone. As fast as it appeared. Closed up!

Jake got on his knees. He pounded the ground with his fists. He tried digging.

Nothing happened.

"Kyle!" he yelled.

He stood. He grabbed the torch. Jake did everything he could. He turned it. He twisted it. Nothing worked.

The ground didn't open up.

Kyle was gone.

7
CAUGHT

It was odd. Just like when the castle fell. Kyle wasn't hurt.

The ground swallowed him up. Then it all went black. He found himself on his knees. He was still in the Secret Caves of Nojra. There was only one way out. The other way was a dead end.

Why am I here, he thought.

Kyle stood up. He looked down a row of torches. He was hoping he could see something. Anything. But the tunnel kept going. And going. And going.

Cave drawings

"Jake!" Kyle called.

He heard his echo. There was no answer.

"I'm never playing *Clan Castles* again! *If I ever get out.*"

Kyle was alone. And scared. He was used to playing this game with Jake. Now he was on his own. He would have to take care of himself.

He walked for a long time. The cave

seemed never-ending. He thought about grabbing another torch. No way! He'd learned a hard lesson. He left them alone.

Who knows where I'll end up, he thought.

He was done. Just about to give up. Then the cave widened. Kyle was standing in front of a huge flat-screen TV. It was ten-feet tall. It looked cool on the cave's wall.

Kyle moved closer. That was … no way! Jake's living room. On the screen. The room they had always played Xbox. This was too weird.

"Hey!" Kyle screamed.

He started to hit the screen. Kyle realized something. His arms weren't hitting anything. They were going through. Like he was hitting a cloud. Kyle could see his arms reaching into Jake's living room.

"I can go through it! It's a portal," Kyle gasped. He could not believe it.

He tested the screen again. Yes! A portal. There *was* a way out.

"Jake," he called. "I'm gonna get help."

Kyle took a few steps backward. He ran toward the screen. Closed his eyes. And jumped.

He landed with a thud. He blinked. Ugh! Still in the cave. He scratched his head. What the …

"What's going on?" he said out loud.

Kyle jumped through the TV portal again.

Again he landed right in front of the TV. In the cave. He could still see Jake's living room. This was not happening.

Three more jumps. Same thing.

"I hate this game," he yelled.

Then Kyle heard a sound. It was low. Soft. But it quickly grew louder. Footsteps.

"Jake?" Kyle whispered.

Suddenly, a woman appeared in front of him. She was tall. With big muscles. She wore a helmet. A sword flashed in her hand.

"No," the woman said. Her voice was low. "I work for King Nojra. Happy to see me?"

"Ahhh!" Kyle took off.

He heard her chasing him. Then he heard her laugh. It was loud. Filling the cave. Surrounding him. Echoing.

He was a fast runner. Kyle used every muscle he had. He spotted a small opening in the cave wall. A place to hide?

He quickly ducked into it. He held his breath. His heart thumped. He thought she would hear it. *Thump-thump! Thump-thump! Thump-thump!*

The big woman with the sword ran by him. Kyle knew he had to wait. Her footsteps faded.

He waited a long time. Slowly he let out his breath. He needed a break. Then he would go in the other direction. Maybe there was another cave. Did he miss one? He wanted to get far away. As far away as he could from this warrior.

He was about to make a run for it.

But a loud buzzer went off!

Bars sprang up from the bottom and sides of the cave. Jail bars. Kyle grabbed them. He shook them. They wouldn't move.

Then he heard the laugh again. Her laugh. The one that filled the cave. He couldn't think. He couldn't breathe.

She had him. He was a goner. For sure.

AHHHHHHH!

8
ARJON

The path was damp. Jake almost fell as he walked. He used the cave walls to steady himself. They were wet too. And slippery. So they weren't much help.

CAUTION

bat goo
ahead

"Do I have a visitor?" an old voice asked.

Jake looked around. He did not see anyone. At first.

He looked in the shadows. Out came a man. He had a white beard. He wore a T-shirt that said "You Only Live Once." It was faded. And ratty. He also wore jeans. They were shabby too. Jake could see the man's hairy toes. They stuck out from his beat-up shoes.

Can I get one at the gift shop?

54

"Who are you?" Jake stepped back.

"I am Arjon. I was sucked into this game too." Arjon smiled.

Why was this dude happy? Jake couldn't understand it.

"I'm Jake. I've been here for a few hours."

"Well," Arjon snorted. "Video game time goes slow. It's faster in the real world. A few hours? Could be a year."

A year? Nuh-uh! Jake couldn't believe it. What did it mean? How long had they been here? Where was Kyle? He needed to keep moving.

"Yeah. A year. But I know how to get out of here." Arjon frowned. "I am just too old. And too frail. I can't make the journey alone."

"You know how to get out? Lead the way, Arjon!" Jake pointed around the cave. "I'll help you get there. Which way?"

Arjon put his hand on Jake's shoulder. He pointed. Together, they made their way through the cave.

They walked for a while.

"Do you still like this game?" Jake asked. "You've been here a while."

Silence.

Jake asked again.

"I love it," Arjon said. His voice sounded different. It was stronger. Younger.

Jake turned and looked at him. He could not believe what he saw.

Arjon was King Nojra!

"A-r-j-o-n ... N-o-j-r-a," Jake stated slowly. How could he have missed that? Ugh!

The king was massive. His human head. His dragon tail. A giant burst of fire came from his nose. Jake shielded his eyes.

"You beat me once. It won't happen again," the king stated.

Suddenly, the cave changed. Nojra's castle. Just like Level 99 in the game.

They were now in a large castle room. Members of the king's court lined all sides. Every king Jake had beaten was there. Plus the others. He knew them all.

The room was fancy. And huge. Gold walls. Diamond ceiling. Emerald floor.

Jake hid behind a pillar.

All the kings teased him.

"Face me," King Nojra screamed. "This is the only way you leave this game."

Jake had never been so scared. He loved this game. But not any more.

"Maybe this will bring you out," King Nojra said.

It was Kyle. He was in a cage. It was hanging high in the air. Kyle looked scared.

"I *really* want to go home, Jake!"

The cage hung above a pit of *liongators*. Half-lion, half-alligator. They were huge. Snapping at Kyle. Trying to reach the cage.

The other kings loved it. They laughed. They clapped for King Nojra. This was his empire. He had never lost. Not in this world.

"You have three seconds. Come out! Or I am feeding my pets a treat!"

Jake didn't think they could die here.

Was he wrong?

"One!" Nojra called.

All the kings began stomping their feet. The sound was too loud.

"Two!"

The bottom of Kyle's cage dropped open. He quickly grabbed some bars. He didn't want to fall! Now he was hanging in the air. The liongators were even closer. They snapped at his feet.

"Ahhh!" Kyle screamed.

"Three!"

Jake stepped out.

"I beat you once. I can do it again," Jake said.

"That was a game." Nojra grinned. "This is real."

One of kings threw Jake a small club. It looked like a stick.

CATCH!

Jake reached for it. And missed. How was he going to win with that?

There was a huge roar. Jake looked up. A fireball zoomed at him!

9
THE GREAT BATTLE

Jake could feel the heat getting closer. And closer.

Hotter. And hotter.

He had no time to think. Jake grabbed the little club. Then he dived out of the way. He rolled. The fireball exploded. Right where Jake had been.

Cheers came from the crowd. Loud cheers. Louder than a tidal wave. Or a twister.

King Nojra smiled. Then he blew another fireball at Jake.

Jake dodged it. But he felt something hot. Fire! It was on his back. He was on fire!

"Ahhh!" he cried.

Jake rolled on the ground.

The king's court laughed. Then they oohed. They were staring at something.

Jake turned. Behind him was a large

pool. It was circular. And silver-plated. There were different jewels around it. For some reason, it was overflowing.

"What's going on?" Jake asked under his breath.

"Jake!" Kyle screamed. "Look out!"

A giant serpent came out of the pool. It had a lizard's head. And a turtle's body. It charged at Jake.

Jake whacked it with his club. This only made it mad.

Jake ran. He ran fast. The serpent chased

him. It opened its large mouth. Then it chomped down. Hard. Its teeth made a loud crunching sound.

Everyone laughed. Then they cheered.

Jake was getting tired. But the serpent didn't stop. Jake had to do something. He had to stop this. Or he would lose.

He spun around. He body-slammed the serpent. Hard. His shoulder hurt.

The serpent went flying. It hit a wall. Then disappeared.

"You did it, Jake," Kyle called. "Hurry. I can't hold on much longer."

Jake turned. He eyed King Nojra.

"Is that the best you got?" Jake raised his club.

"No. Not even close!" King Nojra laughed.

The king's court laughed too.

Oh no! Jake realized the game was not

over. Not yet.

Yikes! he thought. *What's next?*

Giant *spiderflies.* Jake fought them. Then he battled mutant birds. Then more strange beasts. And still more …

DEFEATED!

He swung his club like a baseball bat. He was getting pretty good. King Nojra kept spitting fireballs.

Sometimes Jake scored a home run. His club made contact. *Thwack!* A creature hit a fireball. And exploded! *Pow!*

Jake was tired. Very tired. This was a

game. It had to end. He had to win.

He turned to Kyle. Kyle gave him a thumbs-up. He'd wrapped one leg around a bar. He seemed okay. For now.

"Jake," Kyle yelled. "The mirror!"

Kyle pointed to the Mirror of Reflection. When you kept playing, it would appear. No matter what. Not even King Nojra could stop it. Those were the rules.

Jake only had five seconds to get it. A countdown clock appeared.

"Five," a deep voice said. The countdown started.

King Nojra saw the mirror too. He shot more fireballs. Aiming for the mirror. Jake had to get there. Fast. Before a fireball hit it. So much noise. All the kings were on their feet. They were cheering. Yelling. Trying to distract Jake. If Jake lost, he would be at Level 1. The boys would have to win back every castle. Defeat every king. King Nojra would be stronger!

"Four."

Kyle was still hanging on. He couldn't do that forever. King Nojra began lowering the cage.

Snap! Snap! Snap! The liongators looked hungry.

Jake ran toward the mirror. The fireballs were flying. He felt the heat.

"Three."

"Ahhh!" Kyle was losing his grip. Both

legs dangled now. One arm hung loose. No!

The liongators were snapping. Way too close.

"Jake, hurry!" Kyle screamed. "I can't feel my fingers."

The heat was fierce. Jake wouldn't give up.

He got it! He grabbed the Mirror of Reflection.

"Two," the voice said.

Kyle was going down. He was hanging by four fingers. Then three. Then two …

"Nooo!" Jake cried.

A spiderfly was coming at him. Jake ran to it at full speed.

He had a plan. He had seen it on YouTube. He hoped it worked.

The spiderfly tried to get him. Jake jumped. He landed on the spiderfly. It tried to get Jake off its back. Right! Left! Upside down! Jake held on.

He flew through the air above the liongator pit.

"One."

Jake grabbed Kyle. They cleared the pit. And jumped off the giant spiderfly.

King Nojra smiled. He blew a huge fireball at the boys. *Whoosh!*

"Hold up the mirror," Jake screamed.

"It's disappearing," Kyle cried.

The Mirror of Reflection was fading.

Kyle held it up. Just in time.

The fireball hit the mirror. It bounced back. Right at King Nojra. Direct hit!

The court was silent.

There was an explosion. White light. Then nothing.

10
GAME OVER?

Jake's eyes opened. He lifted his head off a pillow. Was it morning?

He saw the TV. He saw the Xbox. He saw the couch.

Kyle was staring at him. He was in his sleeping bag.

They were back in Jake's living room!

They made it home!

"Was that a dream?" Kyle asked.

"The same dream? Both of us? How?" Jake eyed the TV screen.

The *Clan Castles* game was still on. It said:

LEVEL 100 COMPLETE!

start game over?

Jake and Kyle moved closer. Villagers filled the screen. They were celebrating. It was a great victory. The kings had lost.

The boys looked closer. The villagers held up two avatars. The heroes. The winners of the game. They were cheering for them.

No way! The boys were in the living room.

But they were also in the game. Tiny video game characters.

"Jake?" Kyle started. "Should we tell your parents? About what happened?"

"Um, don't think so," Jake said. "What now?"

"We're not playing *Clan Castles* again. No way. No how."

"Yeah. You're right. Let's cool it on Xbox," Jake said. "Man, never thought I'd say that."

He hit the TV power button. The screen went blank.

"How about a nice game of chess?" asked Kyle.

safer game!

"Game on!" said Jake.

Bruce County Public Library
1243 Mackenzie Rd.
Port Elgin ON N0H 2C6